Table of Contents

From the Farm

Cam loves cheese!

Where does it come from?

grass

Cows!

They eat grass or hay.

5

Cows make milk.
It is in their udders.
Cool!

milk

udder

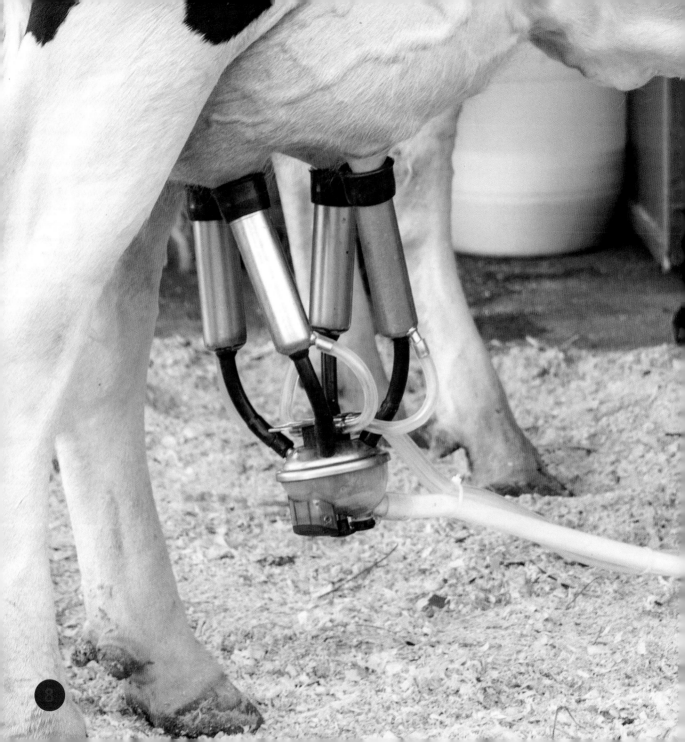

Machines milk the cows.
Neat!

Trucks pick up the milk.
They keep the milk cold.

truck

milk

vat

Milk goes to a factory.
It goes in big vats.

factory

Curds form.

curds

whey

Whey is drained.

This cheese is made into blocks.

It is wrapped.

Nice!

cheese
block

17

Trucks take it to stores.

We pick the kind we like.

We make sandwiches.
Yum!

From Farm to Table

How does cheese get to our tables?

1. Cows eat grass or hay.

2. Cows are milked.

3. Trucks bring milk to factories. Ingredients are added.

4. Curds form. Whey is drained. Cheese is made into blocks and wrapped.

5. Cheese is sold in stores.

6. We eat it!

Picture Glossary

curds
Solid pieces
of cheese.

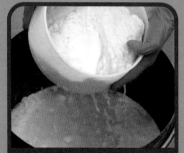

drained
Removed the liquid
from something.

factory
A building where
products are made
with machines.

hay
Long grass that
is dried and used
as food for farm
animals.

vats
Large tanks.

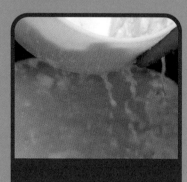

whey
Liquid that remains
when curds form.

Index

To Learn More

Finding more information is as easy as 1, 2, 3.

❶ Go to www.factsurfer.com

❷ Enter "fromcowtocheese" into the search box.

❸ Choose your book to see a list of websites.

Ideas for Parents and Teachers

Bullfrog Books let children practice reading informational text at the earliest reading levels. Repetition, familiar words, and photo labels support early readers.

Before Reading

- Discuss the cover photo. What does it tell them?

- Look at the picture glossary together. Read and discuss the words.

Read the Book

- "Walk" through the book and look at the photos. Let the child ask questions. Point out the photo labels.

- Read the book to the child, or have him or her read independently.

After Reading

- Prompt the child to think more. Ask: Do you eat cheese? Have you ever thought about where it comes from?

Bullfrog Books are published by Jump!
5357 Penn Avenue South
Minneapolis, MN 55419
www.jumplibrary.com

Copyright © 2021 Jump! International copyright reserved in all countries. No part of this book may be reproduced in any form without written permission from the publisher.

Library of Congress Cataloging-in-Publication Data

Names: Nelson, Penelope, 1994– author.
Title: From cow to cheese / Penelope S. Nelson.
Description: Minneapolis, MN: Jump!, Inc., 2021.
Series: Where does it come from?
Audience: Ages 5–8. | Audience: Grades K–1.
Identifiers: LCCN 2019053325 (print)
LCCN 2019053326 (ebook)
ISBN 9781645275299 (library binding)
ISBN 9781645275305 (paperback)
ISBN 9781645275312 (ebook)
Subjects: LCSH: Cheese--Juvenile literature.
Cheesemaking--Juvenile literature.
Dairy products--Juvenile literature.
Classification: LCC SF271 .N395 2021 (print)
LCC SF271 (ebook) | DDC 637/.3--dc23
LC record available at https://lccn.loc.gov/2019053325
LC ebook record available at https://lccn.loc.gov/2019053326

Editor: Jenna Gleisner
Designer: Anna Peterson

Photo Credits: Hue Ta/Shutterstock, cover (left); GlobalP/iStock, cover (right); Guitar photographer/Shutterstock, 1; Lydia Vero/Shutterstock, 3; Lapina/Shutterstock, 4 (boy); Africa Studio/Shutterstock, 4 (cheese); smereka/Shutterstock, 5, 6–7, 22tl; New Africa/Shutterstock, 6; igorsm8/Shutterstock, 8–9, 22tr; Grant Heilman Photography/Alamy, 10–11, 22mr; Ainara Garcia/Alamy, 12–13, 23bm; BeautifulBlossoms/Shutterstock, 13, 23tr; Juliedeshaies/Dreamstime, 14, 23tl; MassanPH/Getty, 15, 23tm, 23br; OVKNHR/Shutterstock, 16–17, 22br; Taina Sohlman/Dreamstime, 18; Thunderstock/Shutterstock, 19 (foreground); R R/Shutterstock, 19 (background), 22bl; Peter Dazeley/Getty, 20–21, 22ml; DenBoma/iStock, 23bl; Jacek Fulawka/Shutterstock, 24.

Printed in the United States of America at Corporate Graphics in North Mankato, Minnesota.

Where Does It Come From?

From Cow to Cheese

by Penelope S. Nelson

Bullfrog Books